# HOT MESS

By:

## NAKIA BOSTIC

# Table of Contents

# HOT MESS

This is a story about the redemptive power of God and His love help set me free from the power of Satan. A story of how I, Nakia Bostic, was transformed from being a Hot Mess for the enemy to being suddenly transformed into the woman God called me to be. There's still work to be done in me. But rest assure I am on my way. I thank God for not being where I used to be. And I am looking forward to where He's taking me. His constant love drives me to want to do and be better. Everything I have and all of who I am is because of God. Without Him I was lost, confused and broken. With Him I am loved, healed and redeemed. This book is for God and His glory. My prayer is that this book reaches many hearts throughout the world, and it shows you how important it is to have God in your life. I tell you no lies, it was not easy getting to where I am now. I've cried many nights and to be honest most days were spent in turmoil because I refused to listen. My mind raced constantly with wonder, anxiety and confusion. It wasn't until I learned the truth of God's word, that I was set free. At first God was a joke to me. I played around with God. I allowed the enemy to clog my head with lies of hate and destruction. I kept telling myself things like God isn't that good or He won't do that for me. The preacher is lying. I did and said some things that I am not proud of, but God still redeemed me. He took me from a place of shame, guilt, hurt, and regret to a place of love, peace, freedom and true joy. God freed me through the healing power of His word. And He can do the same for you. Don't let anyone tell you otherwise. Get to know Him for yourself and see. The enemy thought he had me from the beginning. He was confident that I would never turn to God. For a minute I believed this as well. I was tricked for a long time. The word says in the book of Isaiah (43:1 KJV) that God had already claimed me. I was His! That was one of the truths that I had learned about God. The more I read His word, the more I understood the love of God. All this time He was waiting for me. As you read my story you will begin to see where the enemy had fooled me. You will get to see where the love of God stepped in and rescued me from myself.

All the great authors begin their story from the beginning. Even God himself begins the bible with "In the beginning" (Genesis 1:1 KJV). I will take my cue from Him. Take a ride with me on my journey to freedom. Buckle Up!

I cannot say if it was a warm, or cold day because honestly, I don't remember. All I have to go by is what mother told me, who shared this story a million times with me. And boy it was a story. My God!! I learned later on that God knew me. Jeremiah (1:5KJV) says that He knew me before I was formed in my mother's belly. Like before I even came into this world, He noticed me. He placed greatness inside of me before I was able to talk or make a sound. How cool is that?

Before I get into my arrival. Let me start with how my mother was going to abort me. Crazy right? I don't know why she told me that, but she did. Rejection was a tool that the enemy used to keep me in bondage for a long time. My mother told me that while she was on her way to the abortion clinic she stopped. She sat down for a while on a statue in Albany's Washington Park to think about it. Thank God she changed her mind. But I get it. She had just had my older brother Jevon, who was only just a few months old. I guess another baby would have been too much. The enemy would say to me, when I got older, that my mother rejected me. Or that she was going to get rid of me. He never said that God wanted me. He always left that part out. The lies  continued from there. And you know what…I believed him. Over time I would try to forgive her, or I would say it with my mouth. However, my actions did not show that. Those words stayed in the back of my head for a long, long time. My mother and I lost a lot of precious time together because of the stuff going on inside of us that was generational. I held on to a lot of unnecessary stuff that made me a victim and never who God called me to be, which is victorious. Anyways

**9/22/1980**

I finally made it into the world. I came out on a fall day at 11:35am. I was born to Ardella Maria Comer and Robert Bostic. A cute, brown baby girl with dimples. I almost did not make it. I would call me a miracle. But hey, that's just me. When it was time for my mother to push something happened. That darn umbilical cord got wrapped around my neck. Where did that come from? The enemy struck again. First with abortion and now he is trying to choke me out. What was it about me? He tried it. God said not so. Jesus! Back to my original thought. An emergency C-Section was performed and here I was.  My mother said that she didn't get to see me or know what she had until a few days later. I guess the doctors had her heavily sedated. She was knocked out for a day or two. I was told that my dad had come to the hospital, or that he was already at the hospital due to a fight he had got into in the streets. Either way he was there. I could imagine my dad smiling down on me when he saw me.

# THE EARLY YEARS

Okay now let's fast forward it a little bit. We are still in the 80's, but let's get to the days that I remember. I will go to 1986. Oh, did I mention that I had an older brother? Yes, I did. His name is Jevon. Our birthdays are in the same month. His birthday is on the 6th of September. He's a year older. Yes, my mother was busy, but she did her best to take care of us. We listen and we don't judge! Okay, so my mother and father had broken up when I was 2 years old due to domestic violence, drinking and cheating. My mom said she left my dad because she didn't want me or Jevon to remember what my dad put her through. My mom was right because I don't remember any of it.

I remember us living in the projects in North Albany. My mom was on welfare. She did the best she could with what she had. In my eyes my mother was doing good. That welfare cheese was no joke. It made the best grilled cheese sandwiches ever. Stop playing! The only thing that I did not like about being on welfare was those darn food stamps. Going to the store with food stamps was not the highlight of my childhood. Having food stamps only meant one thing, we were poor. I hated being poor.

For quite a while it was just my mother, my brother and me. Eventually my mother met a new guy named James. He was a nice dude, and he cooked the heck out of some fried chicken. So, he had my vote. Jevon did not like him. James tried to be Jevon's friend. That almost never worked. I felt bad for James when Jevon would give him the cold shoulder. Our father barely came around. Weeks and months would go by without us seeing him. Most times when my dad did come by, he would either be high off drugs or drunk. We would still be happy to see him. After a while that I stopped caring whether he came by or not. Jevon and I would get into fights when we were waiting for my dad to come by. I would make a comment like "dad isn't coming" or something like that. The next thing you know, we were in a full out fight. My mom hated it when my dad said he was coming over. Jevon would be in the house all day waiting for him. After a while I gave up on caring whether he came or not. I protected myself by allowing my heart to grow cold. I wanted to be a daddy's girl. His absence wouldn't allow me to be that. I began to close myself off to my father. I liked James. So, I tried to fill the void the best way I could. James had a son named Damond who was cool. Damond stayed with his mother and would come over on the weekends. He was a little older than me by a few months. His birthday was in February. Damond was my guy. When he came over, he always brought over his toys. I loved that. Now my Barbies also has someone to play with. Jevon had his own friends. I tried to hang out with Jevon, but he always wanted to leave me in the house. He would cry if he had to hang out with his sister. Like what? I was a nice little sister. Leaving me in the house was insane. Nope I would follow right behind him until I heard my mother call my name. Snitch! No, I loved my brother Jevon. But the fact that I couldn't hang out with him was just simply ridiculous. Who was he? I just wanted to hang out. I was only 6 years old then, so I didn't care. Most of the time I spent sitting in my own front yard playing with my Barbie dolls or chilling with some other little girls from the neighborhood. My mother always made sure that I was right where she could see or hear me.

In the mid 80's life wasn't perfect, but everyone seemed to be okay. To my understanding times were tough. My mother wasn't working. She volunteered at our school though. She was well known at Public School #20. All the neighborhood kids knew her. There were always kids at our house. Kids were either in our front yard playing basketball or in the house playing video games. My mother did her best to make sure she knew where we were at all times. We were on welfare, but so was everyone else. After all it was the projects. I knew early on in my life that most adults settled for the easy or simple life. Living in the projects was a trap. The rent was paid by the government or next to nothing. My mother had a whole degree in accounting and was on welfare. How does that happen? I witnessed adults settling. I knew from a young age that there had to be more to life than this. One day I was going to show my family how to really live. No one really strived for or was working towards anything in particular. Just settling. I used to wish that someday my mom or even my dad would get it together and show their kids a better way. I guess life happened. It was easier to settle than to be great. My mom stayed in the projects and my dad stayed on drugs. My mom would let me, and Jevon know whenever my dad was in jail, which back then, was quite often. I hated going to see my dad in jail.  It would take me years to tell my dad how I really felt about his absence. I missed him so much. I wanted him to take me places and do things that dads did with their daughters. He was supposed to be my guy. The man that I could depend on. I did not want any other man other than my father. For his own selfish reasons, he did not show up for me. I felt so alone without my dad. James being around lessened the blow of disappointment. Don't get me wrong, James was a good man. But my dad was who God chose for me. I needed him. Every day that he was not there felt like a sharp sword was being pushed into my heart over and over again. James did his best to help my mother take care of me and my brother. James and my mom had been together for a few years. They claimed to love each other. I used to think that they hated each other. Man could they argue and fight. One minute they were in the room doing whatever. Making all sorts of noise. I guess that's how my little brother came to be. It was serious. They did not care whether the kids were up or not. Most times I would hear everything.  It was their time, and that's all that mattered. After that ended, bottles and dishes were heard smashing against the wall.  James would run quickly away from my mom before the next thing was thrown. How did it go from that to that in minutes? If my mom wasn't fussing at James, it was with one of us. Sometimes I would sit in my room confused. Is that what love was? Arguing, fighting and just having sex? What did James do that made her so mad? Sometimes James tried to argue and fight back. He just wasn't that type of man. I respected him for that alone. I don't think I could have done it though. I wondered why he never got upset to the point of knocking her head clear across the room. But hey that's love. Or so they called it. It didn't seem like love to me. Not the way that my mom talked to James. Even I wanted to fight her after hearing some of the stuff she called him. Calling him out of his name was her favorite thing to do. She did that to all of us, especially me. Her favorite name to call me was Ugly. She would say that when I cried, I was ugly or that I was being ugly when I got into it with one of my brothers. She never called my brothers ugly. All I heard was the word Ugly, nothing else. That word stuck to me like a dirty band-aid. If that's how my mother saw me, I could only imagine how other people saw me. Ugly, ugly, ugly. There was so much hate and animosity in my house. Whenever my mother got mad the insults would coming flying. Nobody seemed to care but me and James. He would leave the house when he got tired of it, while little old me would cry. Her words stung. I tried my best to stay out of her way. Sometimes it worked. Sometimes it did not. I wondered how I survived. Whoever said sticks and stones may break your bones, but words never hurt was a liar. Words do hurt. They hurt you down to the bone. I grew up believing that I was ugly. And nobody wanted an ugly person, right? I noticed that even when I played with my friends that only the cute girls got the boyfriends. Most of the time I was by myself. My friends would come over from time to time. When boys were outside, I stayed to myself. They did not want to play with me. Some of them said it to my face and others just refused to play with me. The word "ugly" kept people away like a shield that seem to surround only me. My friends could play with anyone they wanted to. I had to play with kids that were different or seemed to have some type of shield around them too. I wondered what they were called that caused them to have their shield up. I never fit in with anybody. Not my family or my friends. Not because I didn't want to. I was different. I loved school and got used to being to myself. I loved getting good grades and being in on time. My brothers did not. Usually when I tried to fit in, I got into trouble. It never failed. It was like God was watching me and was saying "No not you" or you can't do what the others are doing". From the beginning I could see that I wasn't like everyone else. The more I fought against it the more trouble I got into. Along with rejection, perversion was also evident in my house. Besides my mother and James having sex all during the day, it was pornography everywhere. You could watch it and read it. They tried to hide it from us kids, but we always found it. I remember one time me and my brother Jevon had gotten in trouble for watching porn. We accidentally left the VHS tape in the VCR. The next day my little brother wanted to watch a movie, thinking that it was Teenage Mutant Ninja Turtles. When my mother found out what we did, we got a whooping and a whole summer in the house. I was tight. Even that did not stop us from watching porn. By the time I was 8 or 9 years old I was addicted to watching and reading porn. Lord have Mercy!

Now allow me to introduce you to younger brother Justin. To this day, if you ask him, he will say that his big sister taught him how to fight. We fought all the time. Way more than me and Jevon did. Don't ask me why, but we did. I think jealousy had a lot to do with it. He had both his mother and father in the house. He was spoiled and annoying. He was my dude though. Let somebody call themselves picking on him. Justin would come right in the house to get his big sister. After that all hell broke loose. One thing Justin counted on was me being there for him. Good or bad. Justin and I had our struggles, but when it came down to it, we were there for each other. We did a lot and we seen a lot growing up in our house. We learned how to survive during the tough situations. Even when were mean to each other we always found a way to make it right. We never stayed mad at each other for too long.

Justin was born on a hot summer day in August of 1986. He was light skinned like my mother and shiny. I wanted to hold him forever when I saw him in the hospital, but that was short- lived. My older brother Jevon couldn't keep his mouth shut and had to repeat something that my mother had said a while back about white people. Why in the world she said something like that around Jevon was beyond me. This is exactly why you cannot say anything around your kids. When it came to stuff like that my mom was not wise. She would say whatever, whenever and did not care who it hurt or offended. This time her words bit her in the butt. On this particular day Jevon decided to repeat what he heard her say. You see me, I knew better. Jevon did not. Anyway, my mother was in the hospital room that she shared with another woman who had recently had a baby. Jevon sees the baby and walks over to the lady and the baby. Mind you, the lady was minding her business. She sees my brother coming over to her and politely smiles. My mother and grandmother were engrossed in their own conversation. When all of a sudden Jevon says, out loud, "you're right mommy, all white babies do have bald heads". The room fell dead silent. My mother was horrified! She was light-skinned, so you know she turned all shades of red. The conversation that she was having with my grandmother stopped immediately. I could tell from the look on her face that if it wasn't for God's mercy and that C-Section she would have killed him. Thank you, Lord, for sparing my brother's life. Man that was a close call! My mother started talking through her teeth and asked my grandmother to take us home. I was angry but certainly did not want to get hit. We left the hospital immediately. Thanks bro! We stayed with my grandmother until my mother came home. Thanks again God for giving her time to cool off. Jevon was surely going to get it. My mom would have tried to kill the both of us in that room. I could never hold a laugh in…especially in serious situations. I didn't think it was serious. My mother did though. After that my mother kept her mouth shut around my brother Jevon. Lesson learned.

When my mother and Justin came home the apartment seemed to get smaller. My room was moved from the front of the house to the back. Damond, James's son also ended up coming to stay with us as well. I guess James and Damond's mother were not getting along. Again, not my story. But if you ask me, I will tell you. In a few days my family went from having 2 kids to 4 kids. It didn't bother me, except for the fact that I was the only girl. Some days, Jevon and Damond would team up to play together and leave me in the house with Justin and my mother. Other days we would all play together. Because I played mainly with boys, I was considered rough around the edges or a tomboy. Don't get me wrong, I played with girls in my neighborhood. I had some friends. My brothers were better. They climbed trees, played with the green plastic army men, made forts in the woods and went hunting for snakes and other animals. Most girls did not want to do that. And who could blame them? You would not catch me doing that now! The fights that me and my brothers would get into were to the death. My chokehold was no joke. When that happened, it was hard for my brothers to get out of them. Did I mention that we also watched wrestling. At any given time, you would see one of us flying or jumping off the furniture onto one another. Screams and cries from one of us getting hurt could be heard all through the house. I know my mother was sick of us. Most of our butt whoopings came from us fighting each other. When my mother had enough, she had enough. We would fight inside the house, outside the house and even in school. Yup we would tear each other up anywhere. And then wait for the butt whooping from my mother. I remember we were in a department store in the mall going school shopping. I believe it was called Children's Outlet in Northway Mall. My brothers and I were running all through the racks of clothing. We were all on the floor. Not trying on any clothes. We decided to horseplay instead. My mother and James had to keep calling us. That was until my mother had enough. My mother took a belt off the rack and tore us up one by one. She ended up breaking the belt and then had to pay for it. It seemed fun at the time to run around the store. My mother did not find it fun or funny at all. She was ready to go home. We had been out shopping for school clothes all day. The belt had to come out. That's how she restored order. It worked for a little while. I can honestly say that I deserved that. I did not get whoopings often. My mother mostly yelled at me. I hated being yelled at. And still do. Some whoopings I deserved and some I did not. Trust me, I was innocent.  For example:

When Justin was around 2 years old, James had a bike that he would ride to and from work. On this particular day he told us not to touch his bike. Did we listen? Nope. I believe I took the bike first and rode it. Jevon also rode the bike. Justin came out of the house and wanted to get on the bike. Jevon puts Justin on the bike to ride with him. I believe they were going down a hill when Justin's shoestring got caught in the spokes. The bike flips over right by a sewer at the bottom of the hill; Justin face hits the concrete and busts his mouth wide open. Blood was everywhere!  I knew Jevon was going to get a whooping. Nope at all. My mom sent my brother to his room. I was already in my room. My mother came straight to me and tore my but up with a broom. Jevon could see the commotion and did not say a word. Never once did he say that it was me that had Justin on the bike when he fell. He just let it happen. And boy did my mother give it to me. My heart was broken but I took it. My mother did not stop hitting me until she heard her friend's car horn blow outside. By then the broom had broken. I was never so happy to hear that horn. She took Justin to the hospital without saying a word. As I laid there hurting. I tried to understand what happened. Why did I only get hit? Hate was definitely brewing for my brother. What happened to him protecting me? James? Anybody? There had to be someone in my house that knew the truth.  Couldn't my mother have waited until she wasn't upset to hit me. I know Justin was her baby, but so was I. Right? Back then I didn't know anything about forgiveness. To be honest I don't believe I would have forgiven anyone that day. I mean of course I rode the bike. But I didn't cause the accident with Justin. Honor your mother and Father. But did God mean stepfathers too? That whooping was brutal. I wouldn't wish that on anyone, not even an adult.

That day went from bad to worse in a matter of minutes. Jesus help me! I can write about it now, but it certainly was not easy.

When my mother left to go to the hospital with Justin, she left me and Jevon in the house with our older cousin. She loved him. They would smoke weed, listen to music and cook together. At first, I was happy when he came over. My mother had someone that she was chill with. She had a friend in him. James worked nights. After Justin was asleep my mother and cousin would turn on the music and light it up. Anyway… After my mother left to go to the hospital my world changed for the worst. I never thought my cousin would violate me in such a way, but it happened. I remember him calling me downstairs from my room after my mother left. He was sitting in the living room with his pants down, stroking himself. Fear gripped my body as he stood up and walked towards me. He put my hand on his private part and walked me back to the couch. I was afraid to move. He turned the movie he was watching back on. It was porn of course. He began moaning as he pushed my head down to his naked private. I could hear my heart beating inside my chest. I wanted to die right then and there. Why was this happening? I was only 8 years old. Clearly not old enough to be doing this with my cousin. My cousin! A grown man. The one my mother entrusted to watch me while she was at the hospital with my brother. Was this my punishment for riding that stupid bike? My eyes filled up with tears as he kept placing himself in my mouth. When it finally was over, I hurried back to my room. My heart was broken all over again. The incident with Justin was nothing compared to what happened to me. That moment changed me for a long time. It was an experience that crippled my spirit. It went beyond my flesh. I felt it in my soul. Disgusted was the only word to describe how I was feeling. Later on, at night more questions began to come to mind. Where was my dad? Again, where was my protection? Nobody came to my rescue. I had to deal with this all by myself. Oh, the hate, and betrayal that I felt paralyzed me to my core. It took a while for me to come to terms with what was happening to me. It wasn't like he did it once or twice. He did it for years. Every time he came over to the house to watch us or visit, he would touch me in some way shape or form. From 8 to 10 years of age he violated me over and over again. If I knew about forgiveness back then... Let me be the first to admit that I wouldn't have done it. And I didn't. Why did I not say anything? I was mad at my mother and brother that day. But not the week after. My cousin never told me not to tell. I guess he assumed I wouldn't. Could he see the fear in my eyes. Or was it my heartbeat that pumped loudly through my chest. This certainly wasn't normal. Was it? Shame kept me saying anything.  As a child I watched myself deteriorate from the inside out. God allowed this. This experience and my dad shaped how I saw men. Men don't love you, they hurt you. They use you and abandon you.  What happened to me made me feel that way. Not God. I was already a tom boy, so my clothing did not change. I kept up in school with my grades. Nothing changed, except me. It changed how I saw myself when I looked in the mirror. I used to like what I saw. After that experience I hated what I looked like. The innocence that I once had was gone. For a long time, I blamed myself. I wore shame and guilt like the plague. If you could see me now in some of my school pictures from back then. I looked exactly how I felt. A HOT MESS. The smile and innocence was gone. Most days I felt like if I did smile that my face would crack. I am exaggerating, but I know that someone has felt like that once or twice in their life.  I did not do anything to stop this man, and I felt ashamed. My goodness! They say God doesn't give you more than you can bear. Ummm yeah okay! This was a lot. Another blow to my chest! Every day that I endured that made it harder and harder to breathe. I wanted my dad. Why did I have to endure something like that?  Being Molested is hard. Back then it was hard for me to deal with. My emotions were all over the place. I did not trust anybody, especially adults. I questioned the people close to me. Sometimes even myself. Did I ask for this? Was this my fault? So many feelings went through my head and heart for years. Anger, Rejection, Resentment and Unforgiveness. No matter what I tried to do, those feelings were stuck to me like super glue. I wore them like they were badges. Could everyone see them? Eventually I stopped trying to remove those invisible badges. This was now who I was. Take it or leave it. Being molested sucked the life right out of me. No one saw me change. I guess I hid it well. My mother still continued to leave me alone with my cousin. I remember when my mother would leave me with my him, I would cry and scream. I am talking about a full-on tantrum. I was a quiet kid. Did she not see or hear me? I understood that she would have to go do important things, but when your 8- or 9-year-old is having a meltdown like the ones I used to have. As a mother, that would have been a change of plans for me. But she never did. She would leave and say she would be back. It didn't matter if I was on the ground screaming my head off. Tears never phased her. I grew up believing that my voice meant nothing. Even if it was a cry. I had to deal with it. Even in my distraught state this man would touch me. Ugh, it was the worst feeling ever. I wouldn't wish that on anyone. This led to my addiction to pornography. That's what he always watched while he touched me or had me touch him. It was mostly homosexual porn with women. Heterosexual porn would be thrown in there from time to time. My attraction grew more towards the women than it did the men. Seeing women have sex with each other as often as I did begin to spark my curiosity. That's all I needed was a spark. All the enemy needed was an invitation. After that he had full access to me. I continued to watch and read porn. Sometimes I would watch it with my brother and his friends. Other times I would watch it by myself. The more I watched it, the more the enemy had access to me. I was a puppet, and he was the puppet master. The only intimacy I knew about was sex. Nothing more. I grew up believing that sex was what relationships were all about.

# TEENAGE MOTHER

By the time I was 12 years old I was pregnant. What a baby? Yup, I was pregnant. Not by my cousin though. This was a friend from the neighborhood. He was cute but I did not want a baby at 12 years old by him or anybody else. I must admit that I liked this kid a lot. But not enough to have sex with him. When I found out that I was pregnant, for me it was something else that would get in the way of me being a kid. This led to me being bullied in school. With that came more anger and aggression. I was tired, but I guess not tired enough. Here comes another blow to the chest. My son arrived when I was 13 years old. I named him Faylon. Don't ask me where I got the name from. I knew I wasn't ready to be a mother, nor did I want to be a mother. This was not fair. I felt like another person got over on me. The guy wanted to have sex, not me. Matter of fact my it was my brother Jevon who wanted to have sex with my best friend. She called herself not wanting to do it alone. In order for my brother Jevon to "get some" he asked me to have sex with his best friend. Was he joking? I couldn't believe that he would ask me to do something like that. Jevon then said I would do it if I loved him. That's not something your own brother was supposed to say. Boom, another blow that knocked the wind out of me. This is what happens when you allow your kids to have sleep overs. A bunch of nonsense. Why was he asking me to do this? I was only 11 years old. I did not want to have sex. What was happening? I believed the lies and went against my better judgement. First time and now I am pregnant. You have got to be kidding me. When I found out I was already 6 months pregnant. I went to get a physical at Whitney Young so I could play basketball in Jr. High. The nurse asked me if someone was touching me at home. My cousin was in jail so no that could not be it. I said no. She said "well you're about 6 months pregnant. Oh my God! What did this lady just say? I am outta here! I put my clothes back on and ran my tail out of the room. I ran past my mother who was waiting in the waiting room. Nurses were running after me. I caught a glimpse of my mother who looked shocked at me running. It was a sight to see. Finally, I was caught. I surrendered and then entered another room off the hallway. My mother came into the room, my head was down, and I was afraid to look my mother in the face as the nurse gave her the news. My mother then started to cry. She then lifted my head up and asked me if I had sex with my brother's friend. I nodded my head, "yes. She then let my chin go. She told me that she was disappointed in me. She's disappointed in me! Well, that made two of us. The Nurse then said she could send me somewhere that night where they take pregnant teens. My mother quickly said, "My daughter is coming home with me". I was relieved. What in the world was I going to do with a baby? Anger, Resentment and Unforgiveness boiled in my blood. I did not WANT a baby.  All I wanted to do was play basketball. And I was really good at it. I still am. Don't play with me. This has got to be a trick or something. This cannot be real. This cannot be my life. But it was! And I hated every minute of it. But for some reason God allowed it and kept me alive through it all. I endured every hardship, embarrassment and obstacle you could imagine. My dad found out that I was pregnant a few days later. James saw him downtown on his way home from work and told him. My dad came directly to the house to see me. I hadn't seen him in years. I remember my mother waking me up from a nap telling me that my dad was downstairs. I remember being excited. Maybe this was all a dream. Maybe I wasn't pregnant. When I got downstairs, I hugged my dad. He sat down next to me. We sat in silence for a little while before I heard his voice telling me that he was disappointed. Tears filled my eyes. After another moment of silence, I got up and went back to my room. There was nothing left to be said. I wanted to scream; dad where were you? Everyone was disappointed in me. No one was disappointed in themselves. Where were the adults? I refused to take accountability for getting pregnant. Adam did the same thing I did after he ate the apple. He told God it was the woman you gave me (Genesis 3:12 KJV). I know Adam knew better, but did I? It was these parents He gave me.  After that school was a joke to me. The district sent me to a school for teenage mothers. I hated it. After I had my son, I started high school. My God! High School was a whole different ball game with bullying. No one put their hands on me, but the comments were out of this world. What would possess anyone to talk about or make comments about anyone like that was beyond me.  Rumors had started about me having sex with my brother and things like that. My son's father and his new girlfriend started going to my school. I stopped going to school. This caused me to fail of the 9th grade over and over again. My circumstances were so loud that it was hard for me to see anything good. Eventually I spent 3 years in the 9th grade. Then a lightbulb went off. I had to get out of this school. I met with my guidance counselor. We both thought it was best for me to leave. I changed schools in the middle of my third year in the 9th grade. I started going to an alternative school. Harriet Gibbons High School. I started school in January. From then on to June I worked on completing the 9th and 10th grade together. Of course I had to go to summer school. The next school year I started the 11th grade with honors. When that school year was complete my grades were back to where they were. A's and B's. Honor Roll never felt so good. I went to my principal before the school year ended and requested to go to summer school again to do some of my 12th grade classes. He looked at me like I was crazy. I remember him asking me, are you seriously asking me to send you to summer school? With confidence, I said yes, I wanted to go. Right then and there he signed the papers for the referral to summer school. That summer I completed summer school with more good grades. I had 12th grade Math and English. The following September I went back to school to complete the rest of my 12th grade classes. I only had 4 classes to complete. I was out of school every day by lunch time. College? No way. My teachers tried to talk me into it. I wanted to be a Pediatric Registered Nurse. All the Science classes was too much for me. I still considered it, but I did not end up going to college until much later. The marathon that I had completed to finish those 4 years was enough for me. At least that's how I felt back then. My son and I graduated from school during the same week. He graduated from Pre-K and I graduated from high school. After my graduation, my son came up to me and said in his little voice, "mommy you did it". I gave him the biggest hug.

# OUT THE PROJECTS

In the summer of 1994, we finally moved out of the projects and into a house. After I had my son, the house was crowded. I was glad when it was time for us to move. James brought his family a house. It was a nice house too. A big three-story house. Jevon and Damond's rooms were on the first floor, Me and Faylon's rooms were on the second floor with the kitchen, dining and livingroom and My mother, James and Justin were on the third floor. It was sweet! Well at first it was. The excitement of moving out of the projects clouded our focus. My mother was working at the hospital now and James worked at a Bakery. Most days it was okay. There was a lot of days where we barely had any food. I'm talking about the refrigerator was bare. If it wasn't for the WIC that I was getting we wouldn't have any milk, cheese or cereal. My heart would ache for things to change. Something had to get better. How did we have a house, and not have any food? This led to arguments between everybody. Nobody got along. Damond and Jevon started staying out the house. Damond was usually at his girlfriend's house. Jevon spent his days in the projects to hanging out with his old friends until the wee hours in the morning. Me and Justin were left to deal with our parents. Eventually we made friends in the neighborhood. It was embarrassing to invite any of our old friend to our house. Everyone was so happy when we left the projects. I wanted to go back. Being on welfare was better than this. What saved us was that every Saturday morning we would go to the soup kitchen in a church by our house to get food. We looked forward to it every weekend. It was held in the church basement. The people that served us were really nice. If we weren't doing that, we would go to somebody's garden to steal their vegetables so we could eat. I hated it. There had to be more to life than this. Eventually James lost his job, and the house quickly faded away. We lived there a little over a year. My mother, Justin, Me and Faylon moved out to a raggedy old shack of an apartment uptown on Sherman Street. Jevon didn't come with us because he was in prison for robbery doing a bid. My mother's job wasn't enough to cover the bills, so she gave up and left Jame and Damond behind. I never understood that but okay. She had to do what she had to do. I was mad at James though. The whole situation angered me. For all of that we could have just stayed in the projects.

Let me back it up some more. My grandmother died before we moved to the new house. I went to Buffalo, NY for her funeral because that's where she was living at the time with my aunt. My mother only took me and Faylon. My brothers stayed home with James. I don't know why only I had to go. Jevon and Justin were my grandmother's favorites. They always went to my grandmother's house. My grandmother and I were not that close. I always felt like my grandmother picked on me because I wasn't a girlie girl. I was too rough for her, and she let me know it every chance she had. After the funeral my mom took all of my grandmother's stuff with her including her old photo albums. When we moved to the new house, my dad came over to visit and was looking through some of my grandmother's stuff with me. I took out one of her photo albums and started looking through it. My dad sees a picture and says, "your grandmother is a beautiful woman". Here's the kicker, my grandmother was not in the picture. I thought he was trying to make conversation. I replied. "Yes, she surely was". He gave me an odd look and said, "that was not your grandmother, she is". James was asleep in the chair in the next room. He was awake now! I looked down at the picture my dad was pointing to. He pointed at a woman in the picture that looked like she could be my mother's twin. I had seen the picture of this lady a million times at my grandmother's house on her dresser. I asked about her. I was always told that this was my grandmother's friend. Eventually I left it alone. My grandmother and grandfather were my complexion. Browned skin like me and Jevon. My mother was almost white. She was very light. That did not make an ounce of sense to me. The lady that my dad had pointed out was the same complexion as my mother. Now my dad was telling me that this lady was my grandmother. And that my mother was adopted. Why lie? Why keep something like this from me? I did not understand. Who was this lady? Did she have a relationship with my mother? And if so, where is she now? I needed some air. I got up from the chair that I was sitting in and went outside. My dad ended up leaving. He knew that I was upset and wanted to give me space. My mother was going to be home from work in a little while. How was I going to act? What was I going to say to her? Honestly, I did not say anything. I was too upset to speak to her. James ended up telling her what was wrong with me. She came to me later on that night. We talked about it. She admitted that she was adopted and that my real grandmother was a pastor who lived in Las Vegas. She said that they did not have a good relationship, but she had her address if I wanted to write a letter to her. I did end up writing a letter to her, but there was no response, so I left it alone. My mother did not want we me tell my brothers. More Secrets. I kept it to myself for years.

Once we moved from our house to uptown it was move after move after move. We did not stay in one place for more than a year or two tops. We always had a new address. After a while I got tired of moving. Why was it so hard to pay the rent? James was still in the picture. Two grown adults working and yet the rent was never paid. Dodging landlords and Rent a Center was the new thing. This never happened while we were living in the projects. Eventually I started working and contributed to the household. I got my first job at McDonald's. I was happy to be working. Most of my money went towards my son. After that I gave what I had left to my mother. It still wasn't enough. But how? I finally figured it out... Drugs! Their money was being spent on getting high. And not just any high... Crack! I was sick of it. I only stayed in the house so I could have a roof over my head. I mean I was no saint but Jesus, crack? The rent was only $300. Couldn't they have put some money aside for the rent? The crazy part was that when I was 15 years old James and my mom had finally gotten married. What was that about? Security? I think not! I was totally over it and ashamed. It was a bunch of foolishness day in and day out. A HOT MESS! Being married did not change anything. It made it worse. The fighting continued. The marriage license was ripped up. The ring was thrown along with the insults. My mother always went below the belt. She had a mouth on her. I must admit that James kept his cool. There were times when I wanted to pop her one good time. I can only imagine how he felt. James would move in and then move out. Every place we moved into this was the norm. We never knew when James was going to be home. My mother was always putting him out. How he put up with that I could never understand. But he did, until he didn't. Eventually he would come home just to say that he was there. But I could tell by his eyes that his mind was miles away. This dysfunction went on until they both started cheating on each other. My mother cheated, but not with a man. She had a woman. I was totally intrigued by this. Sometimes when my mother would stay at her house, I would go with her. Just like with James, I heard them having sex. I had a lot of questions. My mother did not care that she was married. When that lady pulled up to the house, my mother forgot her household. Me and Justin witnessed all of this. Justin turned to gangs. He made it known that the gang was his family. Like my mother I turned to women. Come to find out my mother had been messing with women for a while. This woman, my mother was full of surprises or should I say secrets.

# WOMEN

By the time I had reached my twenties all hell had broken loose. I did not care about anything. Jevon was in and out of prison, Justin was doing his thing in the streets. We didn't hang out that much, but we were still very close. Damond had moved out and had started having kids of his own. What was I doing? Selling drugs and messing with women. Crazy right? I would say so. I was a mother, a drug dealer and a homosexual. A HOT FREAKING MESS. My heart was so hardened at this point that nothing could stop me from destroying myself. Truth be told I was on a clear path to destruction. I was determined not to be like my parents. And I wasn't. I was worse. I worked a full-time job, but the money was not enough. I was tired of being around brokenness. Tired of moving and not having anything. I wanted to be loved; have money and nice things like I saw on tv. I moved in with my girlfriend and sold drugs with her. The money was coming in and going out on things that I wanted to buy for my place and for my son. I was convinced that what I had and who I was wasn't enough. At first it was cool, but then I got pulled over by the cops. I was on my way from getting more drugs to sell when I was pulled over. They had me get out of the car. I stuffed the drugs in a washcloth that was on the door. The cops searched the car and found nothing. My heart never pounded so much in my life. Someone was looking out for me that night. Because nothing was found. The cops and I had a couple of run-ins before I eventually stopped my nonsense. At least at that address. I was pulled over twice. One day a cop came to my house and simply told me to shut it down. My dad heard about me selling drugs and said something to me that I will never forget. He said, "you'd rather make a slow nickel than a fast dollar". That made so much sense to me. After that I moved back downtown. I did not learn my lesson. I got arrested. My girlfriend and I fought this girl over a stolen credit card. The cops arrested us. It was the most humiliating situation in my life. Being arrested, getting your picture and fingerprints taken is by far one of the lowest situations you can be in. I vowed to never do that again. To this day that was the first and last time I was arrested. It's not even on my record anymore. THANK GOD! Once again God came through. Right? After that ordeal I started going to church. It wasn't like every Sunday, but off and on or if they were having a special event. The part of church that I loved was when I went to Junior Church. That's where I met my pastor. Dr. Paul Parsons Sr. I liked how he taught the word of God to where I could understand. He broke it down in ways that made sense to me. More importantly he didn't judge me. I wore whatever. But mostly baggy jeans and a shirt because that's what I was comfortable in. Come to find out it was my family's church. Wilborn Temple. Even still older saints looked at me weird. Was it because of what I had on or my lifeless facial expressions? I acted like I did not want to be there. But I knew that I needed something. I did not know what or who it was, but something had to give. I carried all the weight of unforgiveness on me and in me. I could feel it. Everywhere I went there it was. Hurt, Unforgiveness, Resentment and Anger. They were always there. Even in the people that I had connected myself to had one or all of the characteristics that I was carrying. I am pretty sure I was a sight to see. The more I went to church, the more my relationship with my girlfriend declined. We would argue and fight like it was no tomorrow. Eventually I got tired of it and moved on to another girl that I was working with. We started going to church together.  We didn't stay together long. I went back to my old girlfriend. The fighting was at its peak so when my old girlfriend cheated, I kept it moving. I continued to go to church but did not change. I did not deal with the issues that were in my heart. I never dealt with the molestation or anything. I just let it pile up. I didn't believe that there was any hope for me. But I kept going to church. Bringing women with me and then bringing them home to have sex, smoke marijuana and drink alcohol. That was my life. Sunday after Sunday. I knew eventually God would get tired of me. But it wasn't that day, so I kept on doing what I wanted to do. I did it, knowing that it was wrong. When my pastor would preach about it. I acted as if he wasn't talking to me. But what about the people who were supposed to love me that did me wrong? God loved me too, right? There I went, pointing the fingers again. Where was God when I needed Him? All those nights I cried, where was He? My mindset was totally off. I depended on the love I got from women to function. They were my drug. I felt like women gave me the power to be in charge. I was in a place where I thought I had control over my life and if I wanted to I could stop. But I didn't. I always looked for the easy way out. When times got tough, I did what I saw my parents do, I moved on to the next person. My strength came from being with women. How they loved and cared for me. I had money, my own job and my bills were paid. My son did not like it. Our relationship was nowhere near where it was supposed to be. I tried to be his mother. As he got older, I turned into his friend. After a while his behavior started to decline. His school called every single day. The phone at home and at my job rang constantly. He was kicked out of schools to the point that he was kicked out of the district. CPS was called on me several times. But I still did nothing but what I wanted to do. I continued on going nowhere fast. As a mother I failed to show up for my son. It hurt him to see me with women. He did not want me with women. He did not want his mother acting like a man, smoking weed and drinking every day. He wanted something that I could not be. A mother. In my mind I kept telling myself that I did not want to be a mother. Why was I being punished with this assignment? His father was in and out of his life. I felt like I could do the same thing. Whenever I wanted to leave, that's what I did. I left him alone. I left him to feel how I was feeling... Alone.

By the time my son was 15 years old he had gotten a girl pregnant. I was devastated. I was only 29 years old and was going to be a grandmother. Upset wasn't the word. My mother had found out first and then told me. I lashed out her, calling her the bearer of bad news. But I knew it was nobody's fault but my own. I wasn't a good mother. The perversion in me had spilled down to my son. I caused this for my son because of my own selfish ambitions. What did I do? I put my son in the same category with all the other men who have lied or did me wrong. Instead of being his mother, I pushed him away. Drinking and smoking increased. The enemy didn't have to lie to me now because I was doing it all on my own. I believed that the way that I was living was okay.

I had yet another girlfriend and went on about my business. Leaving my son completely behind as if he did not matter. He needed my love and guidance. Not my unforgiveness and resentment. And certainly not my rejection. He was a part of me. So why did I do that? Why did I turn away from him?

# TABLES TURNED

The year 2009 was a very interesting year for me. I met my maternal grandmother for the first time, my granddaughter was born, and my mother had a massive brain aneurysm. Not in that order. But you get my drift.

I met my grandmother in the summertime at our annual family reunion. I had started going a few years prior to meet my mom's side of the family. The Parson family was huge, and it branched off to many other different families of people. The reunions were huge and appeared to be a big deal. Some people I knew, but many I did not. The years that I went, my aunt prayed and then spoke about our family's history. What interested me most was we had a lot of pastors in my family. Not only were there a lot of pastors, women and men, in my family but some had their own churches all over the USA. One thing that was for certain was that my family was about God's business. If they didn't own a church they belonged to one. That year Justin had finally found out about my grandma and wanted to meet her too. So, we all went to Central Park in Schenectady, NY to meet her. We all gave her hugs and talked for a little while before continuing on with the festivities. I was sitting with my grandmother when she asked me to come visit her in California for Thanksgiving. Was she playing? I would love to. Before then I had never been on a plane. I was so excited. I don't remember my mother being excited. Was it because she only asked me? Wait, why did she only ask me? I became skeptical of this but decided to go anyway. I had to see this through. You would not believe the nonsense I went through because I said yes. Me and my son's father got into an argument over this, my mother was not happy about it and then my son got into a fight and got his jaw broken with a brick. This happened a week before I was supposed to fly out. My son's father asked me if I was still going to go after that. My answer was still yes. For some reason I could not say no. As I stood in the emergency room watching my son in the hospital bed. The pillow that his head was on was stained with the blood from his mouth. My heart ached to hug him. To at least let him know that I loved him. I couldn't. Anger had overtaken me. Disappointment filled my blood. I did not say those words to him, but I sure as heck felt them. I wanted to love my son. To be a mother. Being a mother felt like weakness. And I did not want to appear weak.  Not even to my son. Before leaving the hospital, my son's father asked me again if I was still going to California. Absolutely! The fact that I had to keep repeating myself was irritating me. Not once did he suggest that my son could stay with him while I was gone.  My girlfriend and mother would watch him. If push came to shove…He was 15 years old. He could watch himself.  His father was mad, but I didn't care. I went anyway.

When I landed in the Oakland, CA airport my heart was pounding. My grandmother, Aunt and Uncle were waiting for me. Excited wasn't the word I would use to describe how I was feeling. I met my aunt for the first time. She was so pretty. She looked well put together and she was very nice when she introduced herself to me.  After I grabbed my bags, we exited the airport and then drove to my aunt's house. When I say that this lady had a house…she had a house. I remember it was in a gated community. If I recall she lived down the street from MC Hammer. When I walked in her house it was unlike anything I have ever seen. MTV Cribs had nothing on this house. This was a mansion. No kidding. The ceilings were high, carpets, balconies, master bedroom, jacuzzi and a kitchen that made my jaw drop. It was out of this world! I did not want to ever leave. How could I return home after being in a house like this? Who was I kidding? This was not my home. But it was where I would be staying for the week. I vowed that I would get a house like this someday and have all of my family in it. Celebrating holidays, laughing and cooking. You know, just enjoying ourselves.  I so badly wanted to take care of my family. It has been my dream since I was a little girl. I don't know why. One thing that stuck out to me was that my aunt and grandmother believed in God for real. The energy in the house was different. There was no cussing or yelling going on. Everyone respected each other. Gospel music was heard all throughout the house. The laughter and love was real. It was clear that the family that I was used to was nothing like the family that I would be staying with for the next week.  We ended up going to my aunt's church. It was beautiful. Going to church with my family was something that I long for. This wasn't something that I normally did back at home. My heart swelled with delight. What was this that I was feeling? As soon as I walked into the church, I felt it all through my body. The excitement of sitting with my family in church, while listening to the word and praising God was right where I needed to be. I only wished I could get my family to do this back home.

As time went by that week I questioned if was supposed to see this. Why was I being exposed to this type of living? Was God teasing me? I don't know if it was to show my family how to live, to grow up in the faith (yes, I was still going to church) or start trying to find my own path outside of my family. Whatever it was, I wanted it. No, I needed it! I just did not know how to get out of my own way. How was God going to fix this HOT MESS? Could you believe that even after experiencing this, I still went back home to do what I wanted to do. My pastor talked to me, his wife, and my mom. I couldn't see what they were talking about. All I could see was the nonsense that went on throughout my daily life. I saw my mom cussing every chance she got, my son was all over the place, and all the other chaos that surrounded me. There was nothing to combat it with. The life that I dreamed about seemed to be only that, a dream. Believing this only frustrated me more. I ran to those things that soothe the pain. Women, alcohol and weed. It kept me calm and in control. As long as I was under the influence, I didn't have to deal with what was bothering me. Even though I knew those things were slowly killing me. My body craved the things that appeared to make life easier to deal with. Whenever I was sober all the hurt and pain came to the surface. All that word, God's word that I sat under. Sunday after Sunday. And was not living one word of it. The goodness of God was a fantasy. That was for people who God had chosen or picked. That wasn't me. I never got picked. Not by my family or anyone else. As much as I wanted to fit in with my family, the reality was I didn't. The victim in me was always thinking... WHAT ABOUT ME? I was too busy having a temper tantrum about my past. I was blinded to the fact that God actually loved me. That He wanted the best for me and I was chosen. I was someone that He had picked. From the beginning. God picked me. Where did I fit in all of this? Why was it so hard for me to fit in? Sometimes I would be in a room full of people and still feel alone. My mind would take me places that people only dreamed about. I dreamed of being in a nice home, not just a house, but a home. Having a cook. Making sure my family did not want for anything. I dreamed about being a blessing to my family. Taking them on trips. Having them experience real life outside of the projects.

A couple of weeks or so after I returned from visiting my grandmother and aunt's house. I will never forget this day. I was walking home from work. A huge snowstorm had hit. My mom and I were sent home from our jobs early. We did not work at the same place. But we worked in the same field. Childcare. Anyway. It took forever for me to get home. The snow was so bad. Inches and inches of snow was everywhere. When I finally got home. I believe a neighbor told me that my mom was in the hospital. All kinds of thoughts were running through my head. All I knew was that my son and the neighbor found my mother passed out in the snow. Me and my girlfriend, at the time, walked for what seemed like miles to the hospital in the snow. The snow was still falling. In some areas the snow had almost come up to my knees. When we arrived at the hospital, my son was there. When we came in, he left. He told me that my mom had a stroke. What is that? And more importantly, how did that happen? I spoke to the doctor briefly. I remember him saying something like "he didn't know what came first, the chicken or the egg?" Was this man kidding me? What was he trying to tell me? I stayed and listened for about a minute longer. After that I walked inside the room that my mother was in. She was sleeping in the bed. I called her name, but she did not respond. She was alive because I could see her shivering under the blanket. I was told that she was going to be moved to another hospital that would be able to take better care of her. I thought all hospitals could take care of you. I guess not. I called James as soon as I found out what hospital my mother would be going to. He sent a ride for us. I don't remember who called my pastor, but he and his wife showed up. They stayed for a little while, prayed and then left. My mom ended up staying in the hospital for about three months. Some days it seemed like her health was getting better and then there were days when her health was not so good. She ended up going to a rehabilitation center for Physical and Occupational therapy. It was a lot. Every day I made an effort to try to see her. In March of 2010 my mother came home. I was so happy to see her. The only thing is I now had to take care of her. When she came home, she could barely walk, and she still had her feeding tube in that needed to be cleaned daily. She also had to be put on a bed pan to use the bathroom. MAAAAN, I tried my best. I really did. But then it became overwhelming for me. When I would hear my name being called in the middle of the night so that she could use the bathroom, it did something to me. I am not and never wanted to be a nurse. But that was my mother, right? Nope, I couldn't do it. She had a husband and other kids. Why was I getting stuck handling this? It was like having a newborn baby all over again. Like clockwork my mom called my name at least once during the night. Sometimes I would go and then change her. Other times my girlfriend would do it for me. Thank God for her…I think. Over time my mom got stronger, the feeding tube was taken out. After a year or so I was able to get a nurse to be with her.

My granddaughter Aviona came on Christmas Eve of 2009. I was able to witness the whole thing. My son was there but he had a weak stomach and ended up running inside the bathroom. It was funny to see him running into the bathroom like that. It was not funny to then have to take his place in holding up his baby mother's leg during the delivery. Come on now!

Aviona came out the same complexion as my mother. I was proud to be her grandmother. She wasn't a loud baby either and was very smart. I loved buying her clothes and things. For so long I shopped for a boy. So, when it was my turn to shop for a girl, I was overjoyed. Hands down girl clothes are better than boy clothes. When I first heard her call me grandma, it was a wrap for me! She could have had anything she wanted after that. I figured then that I had to be serious about changing my life because I didn't want my granddaughter to see me growing up in that life. It made sense to just cut everyone off. The problem was I had no clue on where to start. I told myself that I wasn't suitable to be a mother or grandmother. Getting frustrated like I always do, I decided to give up trying. My pastor knew where to start though. He came to my house and took my girlfriend and her things out of the house. I don't remember why he did that. I mean like all of her stuff too. Who was this man? He was family yes, but dang! Was he trying to ruin my life? Or save it? I came to the conclusion that he was trying to ruin my life. I got right on the phone after he left and called her to come back. Oddly enough she did. She didn't bring her stuff back though. We were dangerously stupid. I couldn't see that my pastor was saving my life. I did not like him for that. Now looking back, I can say that I love him for doing that. He was trying to save my life. I was so blinded by what I wanted that I saw him as just another man. Not a man that was trying to save my soul.

My pastor's wife Marva Parsons was no joke either. A gangster for Jesus. One day I had gotten into a fight with one of my old girlfriends. My mother called her, and she came down to the house with the quickness. She was not happy when she showed up. I will never forget what she said to me. This lady was no joke and gave it to me straight with no chaser. I don't know if she was supposed to say what she said…but she said it. You will have to ask me in person what she said. Trust me when I tell you, it doesn't get more real than that. My pastor and his wife reminded me of the man in the bible who had 100 sheep. One was lost. He left the 99 to go find it (Luke 15:4-6). She and her husband did everything to help me. It seemed to fall on deaf ears. I don't believe that I wanted to be found or that I needed it. Still, I continued to go to church. Each Sunday I left the same way I came. Smoking, drinking and on top of that I was a homosexual. I was causing other women to sin. I thought nothing of it. My pastor and his wife used to say that their blood will be on my hands because I knew better. I would say to myself these women are in the church as well. All the girls I was involved with went to the same church. Matter of fact I brought them there. Crazy and hypocritical right? A snowball going straight to hell. Back then church wasn't a place where I met God. It was a place where I met broken women. I met women that had the same issues as me. I met women who struggled with rejection, resentment and unforgiveness. Those were the women who wanted to be loved in any capacity. It didn't matter if I was a woman. I was able to shape myself into the person they needed, which made me feel valued. When I was with them all my issues seemed to fade away. I was able to push my feelings down into my gut until it felt like it was no longer an issue. I knew all along they were still there, I just found a way to disguise them. Unforgiveness showed the most in my relationships. It didn't take much for its head to surface. Whenever something went wrong, like an argument or I felt betrayed unforgiveness popped his head up. Unforgiveness had me in a chokehold for years. It was easy to say that I forgave people, but my heart was far from what I was saying. I didn't believe myself when I said it, so I know that nobody else believed me. Let alone God. I knew a little bit of the word but not nearly enough with all that my pastor had been preaching and teaching. I was going to church just to say that I was going. Wasting time. I wanted to be whole. Doing what it took to be whole was different story. What does it say? Having a form of godliness but denying the power thereof. Yeah, that was me. It was many times that my pastor would see me outside of church smoking and drinking. He never said anything. I felt convicted, but not enough to stop doing it. I had to be convicted by God, not my pastor. And I wasn't there yet.

For years, church was a place that I went to on Sunday to appear to others that I had my head on straight. I could act like a "church girl". But underneath it all it was just a disguise. A look that I put on so that people would find some type of value in me. Inside I was hurting. Deeply wounded from past trauma, hurt and pain. I put the blame on the devil, not knowing or understanding that some of it I caused myself. I refused to take accountability for the trauma, hurt or pain that I had caused to others. It was the devil. I had to have someone to blame so that I could continue to do what I wanted to do. As long as I was able to dress it up on the outside, I was good. In my relationships I was the problem. I put on a good front to get what I wanted. I refused to deal with the little girl in me. What was the point? The damage was already done. In the end I stole from them what I believed was stolen from me. I took valuable things like peace and love. I wasted their time. We would break up and I called myself looking for the next victim. Sometimes while I was in a relationship, I was looking for another woman just in case that didn't work out. Some relationships got violent. I wasn't proud of that. Sometimes I felt like I needed to go there to express my so-called love. All of the relationship ended in weird ways. To this day, most of them I am not friends with. Today I can gladly say that I am so happy that none of those relationships went very far. Even when Obama passed that same-sex marriage, I knew better than to do that.

As time went on, because of those failed relationships my life spiraled. My level of not caring for anything or anyone increased. My son and my relationship was almost non-existent. Days would go by without us seeing each other. He would either be at his girlfriend's or father's house. I would miss him, but not enough to care if he was okay. In my mind I was finally at the place where I didn't have to be a mother. He could watch after himself. Those days were over. I was free! Or was I?

Many nights I went without sleep. Tossing and turning. The guilt of everything began to wear on me.  Praying for things in my life to change but still not accepting that I had to change, in order for my life to change. My pastor used to say that I was one decision away from my life changing. His words went right over my head. Even if I made a decision to make him happy my heart was not in it. I had a head knowledge of God. My heart wouldn't go near God. I wouldn't allow myself to get out of my own head. Pain was my protection. Who was I without my pain?  Healing meant that I would have to let some stuff and people go. I wasn't ready for that. Everywhere I looked there were my wounds. And the only way to heal the pain was by loving a woman, taking a drink or smoking. I coped with the lost, the hurt and betrayal by getting to the place where I didn't feel anything. It was like putting a band aid on a gunshot wound. Eventually my blood would spill out and I would be exposed.  I covered everything up and changed the bandages as often as possible. No one could see me bleed. All this stuff seemed to heal the pain. I was numb to the point where I didn't feel anything. Not even the things I was supposed to feel. The more I tried to get away from everything, the worse it got. I would always find myself back in the arms of a woman, having another drink or smoking some weed. I would tell myself that I did not like who I was, but I did absolutely nothing to change it. After a while I knew I wasn't fooling anyone but myself. I don't care how much word I knew, if I wasn't living any of it, what was the point?

In 2013 I decided to leave women and weed alone. I found myself with this guy who I thought I loved. I met him in February. By my birthday he asked me to marry him. That was quick! During that time, leading up to my birthday was terrible. I fought with this man day in and out. I had no respect for him. I moved in with him and things got worse. The fighting turned physical. Most days I didn't know what were fighting about. We just fought. It was embarrassing. It was embarrassing for me because I actually started to love him. I was in a relationship with a man that I didn't know how to deal with. I was so used to being in charge that it was hard for me to let my guard down to love him the way that he deserved. I did in his house what I saw my mother do in her house. I argued, cussed and fought him about everything. This man didn't stand a chance and that wasn't fair to him. When I decided to leave him, it hurt me. In my mind it was another failed relationship. This one hurt differently though. It hurt because I couldn't manage it. I wasn't able to be the woman he needed. It hurt like crazy. It was hard for me to show him the softer side because I was hard for so long. It scared me when he told me that he love me and wanted to be with me. I pushed him away because I was uncomfortable. I went back to women where I was more comfortable. I told myself that God did not want to be with a man.

Later on, that year my stepbrother Damond passed away. I spoke to him briefly the night before he passed. I ended up putting him on hold to take another call. He hung up on his end. I sent him a text telling him that I loved him. That was the last time I spoke to him. When my stepbrother passed it tore a small hole in me. Damond was the brother that I talked to about whatever. My first male best friend was Damond. We would laugh and talk for hours, in person or on the phone. I felt lost when he passed. After that I tried to hold on to everyone else in my life as tightly as I could. Even the people who didn't belong in my life I held on to. Two months later in 2014 my son's father passed away. I got the news that he passed while I was leaving bible study. My heart felt like it came out of my chest. When I went to the hospital he was still on the back board of the stretcher. A breathing tube was hanging out of his mouth. My son was sitting next to him holding his lifeless hand. Before leaving the hospital, I leaned over and gave my son's father a kiss on his cheek. I whispered "goodbye" and left. For the sake of my son, I kept my cool. I wanted to fall on the floor and cry. I wanted to shout to God that this wasn't fair. Over the years my son's father and I had become cool. The deaths that I was experiencing was hitting too close to home. Two important men in my life were gone. God knew that I needed them. He allowed them to be taken. The crazy thing about it was they has passed away from the same thing. A pulmonary embolism. They had gotten them differently. The end result was the same. I knew that it was only a matter of time before I would be next. I just knew that God wouldn't spare me much longer. What reason would He have to continue to keep me alive for? I was not getting any better. The only thing that had changed was that I had decided to go to college. My major was Adolescent Education. I pushed myself to believe in myself and to get a degree. That did not happen! I switched up my degree before the cutoff point to Human Services. That degree I did complete with honors. One of the proudest days of my life. Both my mom and dad were there. It took a lot for me to get to that place. My son father passed away during my first semester. I was still dealing with the passing of my stepbrother. My car malfunctioned on me, halfway through my 2nd semester. I kept going though. I was working then as a bus driver for the Albany School District. My supervisor allowed me to take my bus to school or to get a ride from another bus driver. I escaped not being able to get to and from school. I pushed my way through to make it where I felt like I needed to be. I wanted this for myself. It wasn't to show anyone but me that I could do it. Initially I started off failing. I somehow was able to turn it around to get the grades that I knew that I was capable of. When my son's father passed away, I did not think I was going to make it. After his passing everything felt like a blur to me. I would sit in class thinking about this man and how it was affecting my son. Sometimes my eyes filled up with tears. I would have to wipe them away before continuing on with my work. I didn't have any friends in college. I talked to people here and there, but nothing came of it. I stayed to myself. Even still managed to get on the President's List in school. I went to my son's father funeral during a morning break that I had in school. In between classes, I had three hours to spare. I cried on the way there and on the way back. Seeing my son at his father's funeral was one of the first times I had actually looked at him and saw pain. Not because of his father's death, but just pain. Life had been so unfair to him. I wasn't there and now his father left. I cried for my son. I cried for all the pain that I had caused him. I wanted to fix it, but I didn't know how to. I couldn't fix my own pain, so how was I going to fix his?

Once I finished college, I felt like it would be smooth sailing from there. Nope! My mother's condition started to get worse. Every time I turned around, she was in the hospital. And now she had to go to dialysis for her kidneys three times a week. Some days she would not go. She would get mad at one of us if we tried to take her or asked her about it. I would do the best with her that I could. Most days I would leave it up to her nurse. My mom was literally deteriorating before my eyes. She had started falling all over the house. She ended up breaking her hip and smashing her face. It pained me to see her that way. I needed her to get better. But what I wanted and what she wanted were two different things.

My brother Jevon came home from prison and stayed with her for a little while. That appeared to make things worse. Jevon was not in his right mind. Meaning that his mental health was off. I'm talking way off. I don't know if it was because he had been in prison most of his life. My brother definitely needed to be on some type of medication. He would go in the bathroom and talk to himself. It sounded like an argument. Then he would hit himself over and over again. His lips or his nose would be bleeding when he exited the bathroom. Sometimes one of us would have to knock on the bathroom door or yell out his name to get him to stop. I felt bad for my brother. This wasn't the brother that I remembered. He was really disrespectful towards my mother and anybody else who had something to say about it. When Jevon got into with my son and hit him in the head with a hammer I lost all respect for him. The safety of son was where I drew the line. I stayed with my mother as well to keep her safe. It was too much for me. Plus, my mother wanted money, and I was too selfish to give it to her. I ended up going into a shelter. My mother kicked Jevon out. She stated that he had become too violent to live with her. Her nurses were afraid to come to the house. Everyone stopped going over there because of him. Most days I would see my brother walking around aimlessly with nowhere to go. Jevon ended up going back to prison on an attempted murder charge. He is now doing 18-life in prison. When I saw my brother in the newspaper, my heart sank. Jevon never talked to anyone about his mental health. Or anything that bothered him. I knew what was wrong. But it is his story to tell. I think about my brother sitting in his cell all the time. I wonder if he thinks about his family and all the time that he has lost with us.

In the midst of this chaos, I would have these dreams. Not just any dream, but dreams that I could remember. For example: One night I had a dream that I was in the emergency room. Everything was white. Nothing was on the walls. I went to the emergency room because I was sick with a cold. The nurse came in to check my vitals and then left out. The doctor came in and told me that I was pregnant. I knew for sure that the doctor had lost his mind. I told him that I was not pregnant and that there was no possible way for this. The doctor did not say anything. He quietly began to prepare the room as if I was going to give birth to this so-called baby. Did he not hear me? Doc I am not pregnant I said again! He continued doing what he was doing. Odd right? This man was losing his mind. How was he preparing me for a baby that I was not pregnant with? I was going to tell him one more time, but then I woke up. It was just a dream! More dreams came similar to that. I always woke up before I could hop down off the table. Later on, my dreams began to change to even stranger dreams.

About a month after I went into the shelter I moved into a room. I stayed there for about four years and then I moved into an apartment next door with a friend. We called ourselves trying to be together. To be completely honest I did not want another relationship with a woman and neither did she. I let it go and became her friend. My feelings/heart began to change. I wanted more for myself. We ended up becoming really cool. Something like sisters. Don't get me wrong, I still tried to go back every now and again to women. It never worked out the way that I wanted it to. I did not go back because I wanted to. I went back because that's how people knew me. It was what people expected of me. Women validated me. Even though I still drank alcohol, women no longer satisfied me. Come to think of it, I don't believe they ever did. It went along with the territory. I remember the first time I sex with a woman. I was so disgusted. I thought if I did it again it get better. Nope! Still nasty. I figured out that I needed to be either drunk or high to perform.

That's what kept my defenses down. I was actually doing this to myself. I was never sober while I was with women. I either had to have one or the other or both. The bible tells us to be sober-minded (1 Peter 5:8 KJV). The devils prowls around looking for whom he may devour. By staying high or drunk I was giving the enemy room to take over. Having sex with women was what I always ran to. What was I going to do now that I did not want to do that anymore? I had a roommate that I saw as my sister. What made her so different? Someone had flipped the switch. My flesh wanted to continue to stay in that comfort. Spiritually I could no longer continue to do that to them or me. I had to have a hard conversation with myself about what I was feeling, the changes and what I needed in order to help me get through this. I needed God. Nothing more, nothing less. I apologized to my friend and asked for her forgiveness. I told her about my past and how it affected it me. I knew then that I needed help. God was the only one who could do it for me. At first, I wasn't able to answer any of my own questions. Who was I? How did I get to this point? What I wanted to do next? And what was I going to do with the mess that I created within my family? My son. How was I now going to be a mother to him? Unforgiveness started to seep in. Not only that but I was reminded of all the things I had done and what was done to me. Anger was back. Where was my drink? I needed something to numb it before I exploded. The more I thought about it, the more I hid in my shell. I had to forgive myself and others. Could everyone see what I was seeing when I looked in the mirror? Who was this girl? What did she have to offer to this world? Why was God allowing me to stay here after I've done so much wrong? The people that I have hurt, the pain that I had caused. Would my family ever forgive me? These are some of the questions that I asked myself. I refused to bring them to God. It was no telling what He was going to say. In my opinion I had messed up badly to ask him anything.

# MY MOM

When my mother passed away in 2021. My life changed drastically. The first thing I thought about was running back to what I was comfortable with.  It was no longer there. My friend let me know that that was not going to happen. I respected it. I had started back smoking. I never stopped drinking, so those were the things I did to help me cope. After her death I drank a lot. It did not matter what time it was. If I felt like I needed a drink, then that's what I did.  I claimed I was doing it for my mother, but I knew better. Drinking was helping me to numb my feelings. It wasn't helping me to get rid of my feelings. It was only suppressing them so that I could manage my day to day. Losing my mother was tough for me. I had never put a funeral together. Thankfully with the help of my family and friends I was able to send my mother off nicely.

I remember the morning vividly. It was the day after her birthday, August 21, 2021.  Justin called to tell me that mommy was not doing so well. He said that she had to be resuscitated already that day. The doctors wanted to know what I wanted to do if she coded again. Isn't that a question for her husband? The decision was left up to me. I got dressed to go to my brother's house. Justin reiterated that, along with James, they wanted me to make the decision. While I was at Justin's house, the hospital called to say that my mother was not going to make it, and someone needed to come to the hospital. I went to the hospital to see my mother. Seeing my mother for the last time in the hospital bed haunted me for days. A strong wave of guilt washed over me. I thought about all the times she asked me to come see her or when I wouldn't bring her over the food she wanted. I was always too busy. The guilt of me not being a good daughter is what popped in my head.  I knew my mother was not going to get better. When I walked in the room, she was still alive. Only one of her eyes was open.  I could see that her heart was still beating on the machine. I almost fainted when I saw her. The doctor said that they had recently resuscitated her. She would go again any minute. The question was asked if I wanted her to be resuscitated. I looked at my mom in that condition for a while and told the doctors that I did not want them to resuscitate her again. Minutes later her heartbeat began to slowly drop down. Tears filled my eyes while I held her hand. I said to her softly that she could go and that I would be alright. I thought I saw her eyes open up all the way before she took her last breath. I gave her a kiss on her cheek and let her hand go. Tears slid down my face. For a second a wave of rage washed over me. I thought to myself, how dare she leave me. Her last blood pressure reading was 9/6. That is Jevon's birthday. He was in prison and had to be told that my mother was no longer with us. I called Justin to tell him, my grandmother and my father. That night I sat down to write Jevon about our mother. To this day I have yet to hear back from him. Losing a parent is the most agonizing thing you can go through. It felt like God was punishing me. I stopped messing with women and then he took a woman, my mother, away from me. Who does that? I did not want nothing to do with God. I was mad at my mom and God. They both had some explaining to do. After everything I went through, now this? I did not believe I could get through this. I fought with God over this. Why didn't he just heal my mother? She was only 63 years old. The day I saw her in the casket brought back all the memories of her. I remembered her teaching me how to skip and how we would race to the mailbox and back to house. She never let me win. I had to run to beat her to the house. We would laugh for hours as she told the story to her friends. I remembered her putting up my report cards on the refrigerator and giving me money for all the A's I got. I was going to miss that woman. Right after those memories came up, the bad one showed up. All the whoopings, the lies she told me, and her getting sick. I cried at my mother's funeral, but not for long. By the time it ended I was numb, I needed a drink and wanted to leave.

I had a dream the night before I lost my mother. A dream that I will never forget. It was storming outside. The rain was coming down so hard I could hardly see in front of me. Then all of a sudden people and huge objects like houses and what not started to blow away. I was terrified! People were running all over the place trying to get to safety. I spotted a huge rock that was sitting under a picnic table. I ran towards the rock and held on to it for dear life. People were yelling at me to run! I refused to leave. I continued to hold on to the rock. One by one people were being thrown by the wind.

Houses were flying by. I was scared but I did not let go of the rock. Instead, I shut my eyes really tight and held on. When I opened my eyes, it was sunny out again. The birds were chirping, and I was alone. Looking around I was confused as to what had happened. Nobody was around. I called out to anyone, I thought would hear me, I woke up from the dream puzzled and asking questions. Why did I run to the rock? Where did it come from? Why didn't anyone else run to it? What was it about the rock that kept me safe? After all it was just a rock, right? Out of all the dreams that I remembered I can say that that one hit me the hardest. It was mainly because my mother passed the very next day. So, I thought that God was telling me that the passing of my mother was the storm, and He was the rock.

# GOD

A few years later I moved out of Albany to Cohoes, NY. I had changed churches. I now went to church where nobody knew me. Nobody knew of my past. I could get a fresh start. The pastors at this church were no joke either. Pastor Tre and Pastor C. They were husband and wife and they both preached. When my old pastor asked me why I wanted to leave his church, I told him that it was between me and God. I didn't know why I wanted to leave. I just knew I had to. It felt too familiar to me, and I wasn't changing. My old church family was going to be missed. I started off with watching my new church online. I loved how the pastor and his wife taught the word of God together. It was straight and to the point. If I missed a Sunday, I would wait to try to catch it later on. Even when I was out of town, I watched it. It took me a while to actually enter the church, but once I did, I went every Sunday. When I made the decision to leave, I knew it was the right thing to do. Once that change happened people started to fall out of my life like clockwork. At first, I was like what is going on. Friends that were once close to me stopped calling or wanting to hang out. It bothered me at first but then I started not to care. I mean some of my friends and family would come to visit, but eventually the visits slowed down. Most days I would just go to work and come home. No visits and no calls. I was fine with it. Even though I missed my old friends. I was looking forward to the new people that God was going to place in my life. If I smoked, I smoked alone. The same thing with drinking, unless I was invited to go out with some of my old friends. Most of the time I didn't want to and would cancel the plans I had. Eventually people got the hint. It wasn't them though, it was me. I didn't want to live the life that I was living anymore. I wanted more! By the end of 2024 I had made up in my mind that I no longer wanted to smoke or drink anymore. I had already stopped smoking. My goal was to stop smoking and drinking for good. My exact words were that I was going to be healthy. 2025 was the year where God would sit me down to get my full undivided attention. In other words, God had a plan and was going to use the changing of the new year to bring His plan for my life to the forefront. Whether I liked it or not, it was my due season. It was my time to grow up in Christ and to follow my purpose. First, He would tear me down and then slowly build me back up the way He designed me. When the New Year came, I went to church like I always do. The praise and worship team was off the chain! I absolutely loved it. During the service I declared to myself that this year was going to be my year. I was determined! The word of the year was expansion. The scripture was from (Isaiah 54:2 KJV). It starts off with a command of enlarging your tent. I really did not understand what it meant until later. But I declared with everyone else that I would expand. I wasn't going to be the same person I had been. Little did I know God was already putting things into motion.

2025 came in with a bang. I wasn't prepared at all for what was about to happen. On January 3rd I asked my friend to take me to the hospital because I was not feeling well and couldn't breathe. I thought I had the flu or something like that. My friend drove me to Urgent Care. I waited for a little while in the waiting room until it was finally my turn. The nurse took my vitals. Blood Pressure read 280/140. She immediately called the ambulance. While waiting for the ambulance she checked my lungs because I was having trouble breathing. She told me that I may possibly have pneumonia. Finally, the ambulance arrived. I was strapped in and taken to the hospital in Troy, NY  I remember one of the EMT's started spraying medicine under my tongue to help get my pressure down. An intravenous line was put in so they could put medicine in that as well. I entered the hospital's emergency room. More medicine was given to me through my mouth and IV (Intravenous). Multiple tests were done. Urine was taken. I was also tested for Covid. This happened until about 3am. By that time, I just wanted to go to sleep. I remember going to get a CT scan while I was in the emergency room. Later on, that night I was taken to the ICU so that my blood pressure could be closely monitored. After I was taken to my room everything went dark. Meaning I don't remember anything. I went to sleep and woke up three days later with no memory of what happened. The 4th, 5th and 6th of January I do not remember at all. I was told that I had multiple strokes and huge fibroids in my uterus. My sister/friend can tell you what happened. She visited me and stayed with me through the whole ordeal. When I woke up on Tuesday evening, I was told that a loop recorder was inserted in my chest to monitor my heart. My heart sank for a minute as my sister told me what happened. She explained to me how my speech began to slur, and I had trouble remembering. I couldn't believe what she was telling me. I came in on a Friday, woke up Tuesday and did not know what happened. The first thing that came to my mind was how this was how my mother's life ended. Would I be next? Changes had to be made and quickly. I could no longer play around with my life or God. I was also happy that He had spared my life. What about my life? My son! My memory was blank. I couldn't remember my life or the people in it. What was going on? For three days I was down. Totally out of it and under repair. Not the hospitals repair, but God's repair. The next three days following I remember doctors and nurses coming in and out of my room to give me medicine and doing tests on me. They wanted to see if I could walk on my own, eat and use the bathroom. To my understanding I wasn't doing any of that before. But I could do it now with little issues. My balance was off a little bit, but I could make it to the bathroom. Physical and Occupational Therapist came in to check on me from time to time. I remember them coming into my room to test me on standing, walking and my memory. My standing and walking were fine. My memory was another story. I had a hard time reading an analog clock or giving change back from a dollar. I was 44 years old and couldn't remember how to tell time or how to give 70 cents back from a dollar. I have never felt so defeated. I was released from the hospital on the 9th of January. I was told that I could not drive or walk up the stairs alone. I was signed up for Physical and Occupational Therapy, along with a plethora of other doctors that I had to see. What was God doing? I had started praying more and reading His word without being prompted or told to do so. I noticed that I did not cuss, drink or smoke anymore. It was like I was a whole new person. I had already stopped smoking before the new year. I thought for sure that after experiencing something like that, that I would run back to it. Not this time. The taste was gone. I had left over liquor from the holidays in my house that I refused to touch. My sister drank them all by herself. The smell of smoke made me sick to my stomach. I noticed that the more I talked to God, the better I felt. Family fell off. My brother didn't come to see me at all. I understood why though. He hadn't really gotten over my mother being gone. The truth of the matter was that I was healing, which meant more to me than anything in this world. Even if I had to heal alone, I was going to heal. I started asking God those hard questions and asking for his forgiveness. I also forgave anyone who needed to be forgiven. Even myself. Relationships that needed to be restored, I prayed. Anything you could think of, I talked to God first before anyone else. God was doing a work in me that would surpass all man's understanding. Even mine. For the first time I wanted to tell the world my story. I wasn't ashamed of my past. I wanted to embrace it and help the next young person. Before I was afraid of talking. My voice was a voice that I felt had no power. Until now! I have so much to say about how I grew up and the things that led me to where I am now. I was asking God so many questions. Even the ones that I felt ashamed about. He was open and honest with me. Even though I was a Hot Mess he was going to restore me to be a healing agent for somebody else. The time that I was out of work was a time of true healing. God started healing the little girl in me before He healed the adult. During that time God had me to Himself without all the distractions. I believe that stroke was not for me to be sick or on meds. But for me to get to a place where I could hear him clearly. I took every opportunity to hear from God. Morning, Noon and Night. I read his word daily and spoke to Him as often as I could. I began to get an understanding about God. The truth was setting me free. (John 8:32 KJV). I was out of work for a while. Most of my time was spent with God. I learned from him daily. Praised and worshipped with him. Anything that put me closer to God I did. My habits changed. I formed the habits of reading, writing and praying. Sticking to those habits is what helped me through and in my recovery. God was doing a new thing (Isaiah 43:19 KJV). Slowly but surely one of the first things that I noticed was that my desires changed. There was no interest in me to return back to who I was. My goal was to move forward in God. I was changing from the inside out. Shedding off the old person was so uncomfortable. Some days I didn't want to get out of bed. I pushed myself to pray in the morning until it became natural for me to speak to God. No one really came around, I began to feel lonely. Even that faded over time. God assured me that He was there with me every step of the way. He wouldn't allow me to get down on myself or to lose focus on who He is. He talked to me daily. The next thing that I noticed was that my attitude towards God changed. I wanted His love, safety and security. I looked up scriptures on His promises and read stories that helped me develop a deeper relationship with Him. The more knowledge and understanding I gained from reading His word, the more I knew that I needed Him. Everything that I believed was bad in my life didn't have the same effect anymore. He was turning everything around in order for me to see that there was purpose for my pain.

That was it all along. It was about His purpose. Not my own. Aligning my will to God's will was no easy task. I had to do the work if I really wanted this relationship to work. Renewing my mind meant that I had to really allow God to reach inside me to clean me out. I wanted to run back to my old self. No way was this supposed to feel that uncomfortable. But it did. It wasn't the fact that He was cleaning me out. It was the fact that I couldn't run from it. I was afraid that if I left God all of this would have been for nothing. I had to see it through. No matter how much it pained me, this time I was sticking with God. The first three months were rough. I cried like a baby. At the beginning of April, I received a termination letter from my job of 9 years. This broke me completely. I have never cried so hard in my life. I remember laying down on my bedroom floor and just crying. I didn't have the strength to do anything else. What was I going to do now? It irritated me because I had worked so hard to get to my position. This was a position that I had waited for. Hurt and anger ran through my veins as I cried. I heard God say, "be still". I hated that I knew I could take these feelings away by having a drink, smoking some weed or calling up an old friend. By then I had developed a relationship with God, and I knew that doing those things would disappoint Him. It wasn't a risk that I was willing to take. I loved Him too much to run back. This is where my faith had to kick in. In order to do that I had to let go and give it to God. I had to give God my worries, doubts and fears.   There was nothing that was going to bring me back to the place of where I used to be. I started to learn that God's love was intentional. Even during my worse day, He was right there with me. I viewed life much more differently. When things got hard, I ran to God. We talked, laughed and cried together.

Having a stroke, being out of work and then losing my job was a lot for me.  I had no job which meant I didn't have any medical insurance. I had doctors' appointments that I could not pay for. Naturally panic began to set in. I thought I was going to lose everything, including my mind. My security was taken away from me without a moment's notice. The good thing was that I could reapply for my position. Did I want to go back? Yes, for the money. Certainly not for all the chaos and drama. I applied for medical insurance and unemployment in the next week. God took some of the pressure off and granted me both. I was excited but also wondering what God had up his sleeve regarding me. I didn't believe that any of this was a coincidence. During the time that I was out of work God told me to write a book. It was a book that I had already started about my life back in 2013. I never completed it. I had given it a title, but God gave me a new one. Year after year I told myself that I told myself that I was going to finish writing my book. Year after year my book sat on my flash drive doing absolutely nothing. I didn't believe God had any use for it. I talked myself out of helping others with rejection, hopelessness and defeat. I failed to believe that God would use me to help anybody.  The enemy had my mind so twisted and jacked up that I believed anything he told me. It didn't matter what it was, if the enemy said it, then it had to be the truth. The word calls the devil the father of lies (John 8:44 KJV). He told me that I was ugly and that nobody wanted me. This was opposite of what God was saying. God told me that I am beautiful, I am blessed, wonderfully made. Once I began to get the truth in my spirit, my fear from people was no longer valid. I could freely forgive, I didn't have to have my guard up all the time, and I wasn't easily offended anymore.  The difference between the book I had written back then versus the one now was healing. I took the time to allow God to do what He always wanted to do and the was love me.  Even though the road was a little rocky, God made it, so I was able to take each step with confidence. With every step He assured me that He had me. I remember when I was doing physical therapy that the therapist would always tell me to hold on the bars when I needed help. She reminded me that the bars were there for a reason and to keep my head up. I believe this it what God was saying to me. He was saying that He is there for a reason and to keep my head up. So that's what I learned to do. I leaned on God and kept my head up. As I became stronger in God the world didn't seem so strange anymore.  Again, I will say that this experience was not comfortable at all. Getting rid of my old mindset, at first, was a struggle for me. It was His that love stopped me from going back. When He closed doors, I didn't try to open them back. Not even to peek at what I was leaving behind. I wanted to live for God so bad that all the lies that enemy tried to tell me went over my head. The enemy knew that his time was up with me.  God was rewriting my story.  A story that I can tell from a place of victory because I know who God is and what God can do. Telling my story was something that I wanted to do because I love to write.  It never crossed my mind to tell my story so other people could be healed. Back in 2013 I was still in complete bondage. I didn't know a way to change who I was or if I even wanted to change. In 2025 God was doing a miraculous cleansing in me. Through the power of His love and word changed me. I mean surely, I had a way to go, but I was on my way. While on my journey with God, I learned three valuable lessons. **I). His love is intentional**. I didn't have to ask for His love, because it was already there. God is not a deadbeat dad. Even when your situations looks crazy, if you allow Him to love you through it, you will always come out better on the other side. **2) Suffering is necessary.** But there is an end. (1 Peter 5:10) is clear about that. It's uncomfortable, some days it hurts like heck, but it's all for the glory of God. The most miserable days of your life can also be the most beautiful days of your life. If you allow God to do His work in you, you will see better days. It doesn't have to be bad. I found it easier to rejoice my wilderness. Don't focus on the how or when, focus on God. (Romans 5:3-5). Take a deep breath and just relax. It will feel strange at first but just relax. It's all going to work out. **3) There are no shortcuts with God.** He is going to get out of you what He placed in you. You can either do it willingly or by kicking and screaming. Either way He's going to get His way. The more you fight with God, the harder it is to get to the blessings of God. Do God, me and yourself a huge favor, stop fighting. It's a waste of time. You cannot not beat God. There are blessings in the lesson. Even while writing this book, that didn't stop me from writing it. I figure if God wanted me to write this book, then He had a plan. I wasn't sure what God wanted me to do next. I had no way of publishing it. The enemy tried to get into my head several times with doubt and unbelief. I still kept writing. Unsure of what God was going to do next, I pushed and pressed on. It was maybe a week or so after I had lost my job that I had gotten mad about my situation. I cried out to God. I felt like He had left me. More lies. He stayed right there with me. I had to remember that like I had said previously, He wasn't a deadbeat dad. God is faithful to finish the work He had started. (Philippians 1:6). So, him leaving me wasn't something that He would do. There were days that I did want to throw in the towel and give up. God even understood that. He understood every feeling that I was feeling. During those moments God became my cheerleader. He would tell me to push or say things like keep going, you're almost there. Going back was not even an option. For so long I depended on myself. Never once did I consider that it was God that kept me through the years. I started looking back over my life and really taking inventory of all the times God saved me, covered me or sent someone to speak into my life that was going to help me. I remembered my grandmother and old pastor telling me to get to know God for myself. I am so glad that I did. Getting to know God helped me with my past. He allowed me to see me. It was when I surrendered unto God that my life began truly to turn around. I stopped fighting Him for what I had lost and started praising Him for what I gained. Love, security and peace. I held on to the promises God. Not my pain or problems. I looked for God every single day. Not because he owed me anything, but because I was grateful. I was grateful that I had made it this far and hadn't lost my mind. Most people would have. Actually, I know some people who did. When I gave it over to God, everything started to make sense. I understood why I had to go through what I had to go through. Why my life seemed so much harder. God had a plan and as long as I was fighting against him my life would continue to be hard. God had to get me to the place where I was able to hear Him clearly. Naturally I tried to fight against Him and do it on my own. Key words I tried. While my mind was trying to figure out what to do, God was simply saying to be still. I remember waking up one morning praying to God. I gave him everything. All that I was thinking, feeling and my worries. I told Him that I was going to trust Him no matter what. God replied and said go write. He said to write about Him and this experience. How He delivered me in spite of me. I then started to speak positively into my own life. I had never done that before. My words came naturally and without hesitation.  I spoke freely about the love and power of God. I know my neighbors must have thought that I was going crazy, but I did not care. I needed God! In my place of desperation and uncertainty, I praised God. I thanked him for everything. I even thanked Him for my past.   God took me from a job where I was comfortable to a place where I had to depend on Him. This meant I had to trust and lean on Him for everything.  I cannot lie; in the beginning I spent more days than not frustrated. But when I began to focus what was God was doing in me and not what was going on around me things got better. I began to experience His peace like never before. God was pushing me forward. He was breaking me down to build me back up. It was in His timing and His way. Before He could expand me externally, He expanded me internally. He had to make sure that I had the capacity to hold on to His blessings. There was a place in this world that created for me to fill. I had to do it God's way.  I was born to be set a part. I had to understand and believe that I couldn't hang out with everybody and go everywhere. I have a calling on my life that excluded me from fitting in. Once I understood that God wanted me for His purpose, I was able to relax.  I was able to allow God to be God in my life. I knew that it was bigger than me. God wouldn't allow all of my past pain and trauma to be for no reason. It was about me aligning myself to His will. His love never gave up on me. On the days that I cried out of frustration were the days that I felt His love the most. Yes, there were times when I was in my feelings, but giving up was out of the question. I fought harder to trust God because I knew that I was almost at the finish line. So, I kept going. When I cried, I wrote. When I was angry and frustrated, I wrote. God encouraged me by pushing me even when I didn't feel like it. Some days I wanted to stay in my bed. He wasn't having it at all. God would say "I had work to do". His encouragement gave me the strength to make it another day.  The door that God had closed indicated that He had something better for me. God didn't want me to be complacent at a job that wasn't allowing me to be what He called me to be. There was greater for me. Initially, losing my job hurt me so badly. I was sad, frustrated and angry. When I began to get closer to God, I understood that He had a plan. (Jeremiah 29:11 KJV) He had a plan to work in me and through me. I just had to trust

Him. I wasn't defeated. Nowhere in the bible does it say that change is easy, but it does say to trust God.

So many times, I found myself running back to what was familiar. I never thought about God. Much less running to Him. My only goal was to fix the problem as soon as possible. When I needed more money, I sold drugs. When my problems got out of hand, I smoke weed or drank a huge amount of alcohol to numb the pain. If I wanted love, I found women who were crazy enough to be with me. The truth of the matter was I was tired. I tired of running backwards. Can you imagine being in a race for your life, the starting gun goes off and you start running backwards? That looks stupid, right? You're never going to finish the race that way. That's how I felt, like I was running backwards all my life. The whole time God is telling me to run forward, don't be afraid of the hurdles, I got you. Crazy old me was running away from the finish line. Running backwards meant that I was running away from what God had for me. Not this time! I decided to run towards the finish line. If it took every ounce of strength that I had, I knew God was running right beside me whispering, "You can make it, one more hurdle and the race will be over". I would push my way all the way to the end. This victory is personal. This is for the little girl whose father left. For the little girl who was rejected. For the little girl who was molested. For the sickness that took my mom too soon. For the perversion that destroyed my family. For the lies that kept my family from believing and trusting God. This VICTORY is bigger than me. This is for the HOT MESSES out there. For the people who is only one decision away from changing their lives forever. A word of advice, stop running back to your mess. There nothing there for you. The scripture says "If God be for you, who can be against you (Romans 8:31 KJV). The fight is already fixed. You win. LET'S GOOOOOOO!!!!!